I am a filmmaker. I grew up in the 1980s in the north London suburbs. Nothing ever happened. It felt like a New Year's Eve, where you know there is great party somewhere, just never where you happen to be. This was unlike the Saturday afternoon movies I'd become accustomed to seeing in the Turnpike Lane Coronet.

There were no time-travelling Deloreans, no extraterrestrials needing a way home, no underground pirate treasures, no heroes and no adventures, so I created one. The I AM is my debut novella.

Robert Samuels
Writer, director, superrocketman

superrocketman

The I AM

Originally serialised as a podcast on iTunes
Published as an e-Book in 2012

First print edition published in Great Britain by
superrocketman 27th March 2013
Copyright © 2012 Robert Samuels

Visit the author's website www.superrocketman.com

Cover illustration & layout by Mark One - markonegroup.co.uk

Robert Samuels asserts the moral right to be identified as the
author of this work

ISBN 978-0-9575959-0-3

Acknowledgements

It's taken a lot of long nights and early mornings to bring this novella to light with the filmed trailers and everything that went with it. The author would especially like to thank: Andrea Low BSc MD MSc, Nic Lawman, Peter Dobes, Jesper Lind, Peter Fehervari, Kip Katesmark, Katy Slater, Elizabeth Osborne, Kelly Owen, Steve Partridge, Colin Wadsworth, Kenneth Colley, Ursula Rani Sarma, Tom Lindsay, Mark One, Nial Brown, Mike Larwill, David Rom, Andrew Kuchanny, Max Herman, Cliff Briggs, Dan Sollis, Kiel Robinson, Scott Marshall, Femi Houghton, Rodrigo Souza, Ricardo Antolin, Joan Hillery, Justine Deighan, Dennis Grasse and my mother and father for all their support.

Dedicated to Laura, one of my favourite Londoners,
you will be missed.

Robert Samuels, May 2012

THE

I AM

Written by Robert Samuels

PART ONE

After the fifth argument in seven days, Hal Maybury embarked on a full-scale retreat to the shed. He'd prepared in advance for this: three kegs of premium lager, four cartons of Lucky Strikes, a four-tog summer duvet, speed dial to all the local fast-food outlets and ninety days of TV listings. Any additional supplies would have, of course, run the risk of interception by Mrs Maybury, also of 14 Clifton Terrace, Finchley, but Hal lived on the edge like that.

"Coward! Stay out there for all I care!" wailed Trina from the patio step. Hal paused, closed the shed door behind him and sighed; but soon the clip-clop of Trina's kitten heels were rapidly advancing down the garden path, honing in on the shed door. He took a momentary gaze at his reflection in a dusty mirror: at his lank brown hair, his grey lifeless eyes and sallow, pasty skin. Over time he'd coined a term for it: 'The Decline'. How Hal hated 'The Decline'. His fifty-two years had not been so kind and his wife of the last two was now at the door.

She didn't even knock: kicking it open 'cop-style', Trina stormed into the shed, dispersing bits of door and splinters across the floor.

"Magda was right! I should never have married you! I

should never have...." But her train of thought hit a sudden, unaccounted for red-light, for in the silent scene of interior shed-night, something was amiss: Hal had disappeared.

He'd discovered the suit several nights before, but didn't remember all the details. Upon finding his marital bed divided, by a small Hungarian-made brick wall, Hal decided to take a stroll. Wandering without reason, destination or outcome was fast becoming a frequent pastime amidst the decay of his marriage. Sometime after midnight he found himself crossing Trent Park Golf Course with a bottle of vodka and fell into a hole, where the seventeenth ought to have been.

"Jesus H!" Hal mumbled groggily as he crawled amidst the rocks and broken vodka glass at the base of the hole. Brushing the dirt from his white shirt and dark slacks, he wondered where he was. He felt tired and hurt, his mind trapped within a daze of alcohol, but slowly Hal began to amass a growing awareness of his surroundings. From the ground, a warm low-lying mist engulfed the area. Wisps of steam escaped into the atmosphere from vents in between the rocks. In the light of the first quarter moon, Hal looked in every direction. To call it a hole would be a misnomer. He was in some kind of canyon, almost 300 feet in diameter with steep rock walls.

His eyes scanned the scene with a sense of unease: there were no excavation machines, hazard signs, barricades or vehicle tracks. Nothing but rock, mist and a faint sulphurous odour; but through the mist, in the distance, something caught Hal's attention: a small white flash emanating from the centre of the canyon, pulsating at regular intervals.

Hal trudged across the hot rocks towards it. As he drew closer, he could see that the light was mounted on the edge of a metal casket the size of a medium-sized suitcase levitating silently at waist height. Hal waved the remains of the broken vodka bottle above and underneath the object. There was no invisible plinth or fishing wire holding it in place. Its smooth surfaces were adorned with complex and precision-engineered symbols and engravings. In all his years in telecoms, Hal had seen nothing like it. Without thinking, he touched the surface.

Instantaneously, the casket came to life; a slow, electronic bleep from within started increasing quickly and exponentially in pitch. Hal panicked, stumbling backwards. A singular piercing tone echoed deafeningly across the canyon. He clasped his hands to his ears, collapsing to his knees, unable to suppress or keep out the sound. He considered his death scene: alone and confused with a broken bottle of vodka, 'flying low,' trapped in a hole in Trent Park Golf Course. It seemed fitting.

It took several minutes of distant sirens from emergency services vehicles, car horns from the nearby A-road and the soft breeze and smell of sulphur for Hal to re-open his eyes. Tentatively, he removed his hands from his ears. The canyon was silent. The casket lay open on the ground with an interior light illuminating its contents. Hal rose, took a few steps and peered inside. There was only one item: a neatly folded, slate-grey jumpsuit. The fabric was soft, rubbery, flexible and felt warm to the touch, and across the surface was a raised hexagonal pattern. There were no wash instructions or clothing label logos. He rubbed his chin in thought and scanned the canyon once more.

It took Hal a while to ascend the steep south ridge; he coughed and wheezed through exercise at the best of times. At the top, he took a long look back at the dark void he'd left behind. From the well-maintained fairway, the rising mist and geology of the sloping canyon walls took on a different significance – that of an impact crater. Hal clung tightly to the casket under his arm and found himself looking skyward, for answers. He knew what he should have done, hand over his otherworldly discovery to the authorities, but instead, he took it to the one place that made sense: the shed.

On the Maybury's back lawn, Trina stood alone in the empty shed doorway, her bright-yellow two-piece power outfit attracting circling insects. Impatiently, she tapped her French-manicured nails in a state somewhere between anger and confusion. Seconds before, her husband had closed the shed door behind him and on her. Now there was just an empty wooden shack with creaking floorboards and nowhere for a man of Hal's dimensions to hide. It was a disappearance worthy of a Las Vegas stage magician. Circling inside the small hut, she clipped her ankle on a metal casket, immediately cursing in Hungarian. Trina hobbled back up the path to the house in just one kitten heel; hoping no one saw her in such an undignified situation. In the shed doorway, the metal casket lay empty and open.

Anderson's Travelling Funfair sprawled haphazardly across the heath; an unplanned collection of second-rate, third-hand, semi-functional rides. In the moonlight amidst the tawdry attractions, music and patrons, nobody noticed the cigarette smoking or floating by itself. The drone of the rides and fairground music eliminated all natural noise, but from within the Hall of Mirrors a piercing scream cut through the frivolity. Jim, the acne-filled Ghost Train attendant, was first on the scene. In the centre of the Hall of Mirrors, curled up in the foetal position lay Edie, a frail French foreign exchange student, candyfloss crushed beneath her ribs.

"W-what happened?" Jim stuttered as he knelt by her side.

Edie's eyes looked through him, filled with terror. "Please," she said, struggling to force out the words. "Get me out of here, please!"

Jim slowly lifted her to her feet, her hands clinging tightly to him.

"Over there, behind me," Edie repeated listlessly as their reflections warped and distorted throughout the Hall's dirty mirrors. Jim was beginning to feel spooked but saw nothing but his own reflection: "W-what was behind you?" he replied, but mentally Edie was all stop.

Leaning against the Helter Skelter, Hal wheezed out of breath. He'd run fifty metres, a Herculean endeavour as far as he was concerned, and his body shook violently, coughing black tar into his hands. 'The Decline' once again, he figured. He reached for a Lucky Strike but there were no outer pockets in his outfit of the evening, the jumpsuit from the crater. It fitted him unusually well, as if made to measure, but he had neither the time nor the patience to admire himself.

"Over there!" shouted several dissident voices from the crowd outside the Hall of Mirrors. In the distance, Edie pointed in Hal's direction.

The mob quickly advanced across the heath. Hal had no run left in him and very little 'walk' either. He ambled around the corner into the deeper shadows of the attendant break area, an alley strewn with cigarette butts, Styrofoam cups and cans of cola. The footsteps of the angry mob were closing in. Hal gasped once more for breath and reached for a small button on the lapel of the jumpsuit. "Please work," he said softly and pressed hard. Hal and the jumpsuit slowly became transparent. The mob spilled into the attendant break area, shining their torches and mobile phone lights into the shadows, but Hal Maybury was nowhere to be seen.

Inside the St. John's Ambulance, Edie sipped water from a small plastic cup, a picture of fragility, her thin legs swinging under the chair, her large eyes focused on the floor. The paramedic had completed his medical examination and had moved on to his accident report, writing 'ghost' and filling out page after page.

"What you saw was probably just a trick of the light you know."

"Non," Edie replied meekly to the confused paramedic.

"Everything alright at home?"

"Uh-uh."

"It'll go no further than me you know." The paramedic paused, smiling kindly. Next to Edie lay an empty report sheet and a biro. Suddenly the biro slowly rose up into the writing position and began to glide across the paper by itself. For the second time, she found herself paralysed in fear.

"Regarde!"

The paramedic looked up immediately transfixed. Letter by letter, the pen wrote:

'Sorry, I never meant to frighten you.'

As suddenly as it started, the pen dropped onto the medical sheet, inanimate once more. Edie glanced at the words, looked at the paramedic; the paramedic looked at the words then at Edie. Both fainted on the spot, their bodies clumsily sprawled across each other on the ambulance floor.

"Jesus H!" said Hal Maybury out of thin air.

The morning after the night before, Hal woke with a start. Was it all a fantastical dream? The jumpsuit? The funfair? Disappearing from Trina? As he lay on the couch he glanced up at the back of the broken shed door and there on a brass hanger hung the otherworldly grey jumpsuit from the crater. Hal ambled over and unhooked it. He was interested in one thing only, the lapel button. He stared at it nervously then pressed it. The suit quickly decreased in opacity until it became an invisible, imperceptible weight in his hand, then he pushed it again and the suit became visible once more.

Pressing the button the previous night had been accidental. He'd never noticed it before. More amazing to Hal was the fact that Trina looked right through him as she stood in the shed doorway, only a few feet away.

Hal slid the suit on and cautiously walked through the garden towards the house, unsure of how he might word his disappearance to Trina. Slowly he opened the patio door and listened. No sound or movement: check. The patio door creaked as he pushed his head in. All-clear: check. He opened the fridge door to reveal a large, succulent joint of leftover honey-roasted pork.

"What do you think you're doing?" demanded Trina standing behind him in an immaculate cerise A-line skirt and matching cardigan. How did she do that? Hal wondered.

"Get your hands off." Trina pushed past Hal, snatched the pork joint, considered her options, before defiantly placing it in the cat's bowl. Hal felt a deep weariness sweep through him.

"Think you're Houdini huh? Well do you? So you've lost your memory as well?"

"What do you mean Honey?"

"You know exactly what I am talking about."

"Just went for a stroll. Don't know how you missed me." Hal tried his best to act normal.

"You think this is funny do you?"

"No, not at all."

"You're lying. I can always tell when you're lying."

"Is there anything I can do right around here?"

"You can think about that while I am at Magda's."

"You going to stay with her?" Hal found Trina's sister unpalatable at the best of times.

"A couple of nights, maybe more, who knows." She looked him up and down.

"You still look like bloody workman."

"I like it."

Trina slammed the front door, her bouffant unmoved in the summer breeze, and stepped into a waiting cab. Tabitha, her Persian cat, attacked the pork in the bowl with zeal. Hal looked out into the street. Sunlight streaked through the window, it was a glorious summer's day.

"I guess it's just you and me," he said looking at the suit. Very slowly, a faint smile crept across his face. Tabitha paused to gaze at Hal with her large, suspicious yellow eyes. His day broke down a little like this:

10:23   Employs full invisibility to ride a south-bound Northern Line train into town; unbeknownst to the driver, he rides alongside in his cabin.

10:55   Takes a walk through Soho confusing passers-by with perfectly timed kicks to their derrieres. The advertising exec with spiky hair, a Ramones T-shirt and suit-jacket gets five for extra measure.

11:17   Takes a seat in a female-only spa. Invisibility ON.

13:30   Lunch.

14:19   Spa steam room: Discovers the suit regulates his body temperature so he is neither hot nor cold. The Austrian Yoga instructor screams, pointing directly at him. The steam has exposed his outline. He looks cloaked instead of invisible!

14:19   Bolts into reception. Hiding behind a fig tree, his large, semi-transparent outline forms excellent camouflage. The Austrian Yoga instructor and two burly spa managers run right past him. He makes two notes to self:

   1: Steam and water can make him partially visible.

   2: Stephanie, one of Trina's Renaissance Society friends, has a far better figure than he had previously accounted for.

15:30   Visits the Meerkat enclosure at London Zoo. Decides to hang out. He always loved those little critters. He didn't know why.

16:30   Leaves sizeable donation in collection box and to Horace the homeless man holding an 'alcoholic research' sign.

17:09   Takes seat in the Caribbean Centre with a group of elderly West Indian gentlemen, wearing suits and hats and playing snap-dominoes. Feels at home here. The laughter and camaraderie is contagious. Finds himself fascinated by the secret world of codes, winks and tics of the domino community and even laughs out loud.

17:45   Elderly West Indian domino players rapidly flee, citing a duppy incident, simultaneously blaming the Ghanaian player for bad Ju-Ju.

17.46   Sits alone with dominoes. Discovers Jerk chicken, sweet potatoes, rice and peas.

18:10   Has two rounds of seconds.

18:30   Feels onset of food coma. Takes a nap in a display bed in the window of the Kentish Town Bed Emporium Showroom.

18:31   Decides a memory foam mattress would be an excellent acquisition for the shed.

18:58   Screams as a postal worker lands on him whilst testing the mattress.

18:58+½ second The postal worker screams.

18:58+1 second The Kentish Town Bed Emporium Showroom worker screams.

19:01   Wanders the streets with a can of beer, some cigarettes and not a care in the world.

19:23   Is almost run over by a convoy of military trucks headed northbound in a hurry.

20:30   Invisibility OFF.

20:31   Sits at the bar of the 'Bandy Legs', next to his favourite barfly, Keith.

23:20   Begins the long stumble back to the shed, sometimes visible, sometimes invisible, but never in a straight line. Sometimes he sings, at other times he forgets the words.

The following morning, the crater at the seventeenth was alive with activity. For the last couple of days and nights, the army had been busy. A perimeter around the golf course had been constructed, secured, enforced by soldiers and, under the arc lights, scientists in biohazard suits combed the ground for samples. A chorus of C.B. conversations and computer processes swept through the site. Dead centre within the crater was a marigold-coloured tent, housing the densest concentration of scientists.

On the south ridge, a scientist suddenly motioned to a colleague. The colleague carefully trundled across, closely flanked by a Lieutenant. Using tongs, he slowly lifted transparent fragments from the ground, dropping each one into a cylindrical container with a red biohazard symbol on it.

"Looks like silicon dioxide," the scientist said to his colleague, who nodded in agreement.

"Silicon what?" interjected the Lieutenant leaning in.

"Glass." Something caught the attention of the scientist. "Wait a minute," he said as he began to tug at another piece in the ground. "You gotta be kidding me!" He carefully removed a larger sample, holding it up for all to see. It was not an alien rock sample but clearly the neck of a vodka bottle next to a set of human tracks.

"We were first on the scene..." the Lieutenant stated confidently, "right?"

From the high-hide amidst the trees by the sixth, a sniper gazed towards the woodland to the north and paused before looking again through his scope. Quickly, he pressed his talkback button: "All calls, movement, treeline, eleven o'clock, Gold team stay firm on crater, over."

"Roger that," chirped the talkback system.

Two snipers remained focused on the crater. Both unlocked their safety catches, curling their fingers around the trigger, scanning for any movement. The third remained in the high-hide joined by the remaining soldiers focusing on the treeline to the north. From the trees bordering the fifteenth, an unusually dense fog began to roll in. It was low-lying, very thick and out of place on a fine summer's day and it advanced towards the crater. The Lieutenant pressed his talkback button:

"Sniper one, send sit rep, over."

"It's coming in real fast, over." The sniper grimaced.

"Roger that, keep visual, over." The Lieutenant examined the fog through his spotter binoculars – it was accelerating. Moving at over five metres per second, already engulfing three of the distant holes and once within the fog, visibility was zero. Hundreds of startled birds took flight. Suddenly from within the grey mass thundered an ominous deep bass tone, like a ship's horn.

"Clear the crash site! Clear the crash site, now!" crackled the Lieutenant over the talkback network. The signal was weak. The scientists scrambled for their lives, haphazardly climbing the crater walls, with soldiers co-ordinating the retreat. The fog was almost upon the crater and began to pour into it. A second bass tone boomed through the canyon, even louder than the first. The scientists and soldiers at the site clung to their ears. The swirling, low-lying fog had all but surrounded them.

"All calls, sniper one, switch to TI, over." The snipers slid their thermal imaging goggles on.

"I've got nothing, no visual, over."

"No visual, over."

The fog swirled; the scientists screamed. All communications were jammed within the swirling grey mass. Those trapped inside found their movements severely restricted. Scientists and soldiers called out to one another for help then suddenly, almost as quickly as it had begun, the fog started to dissipate, retreating back through the woodland. The sniper in the high-hide stared through the clearing mist at the crater. He pressed his talkback button which crackled, but as the mist began to ease, communication was restored.

"All calls, get visual on the seventeenth; you're not going to believe this."

"Roger that. I see it... I don't believe it!" replied a solider in the course rough.

Where seconds before there was a vast impact crater, now there was an immaculately pristine seventeenth hole in the golf course. It was like it never happened.

The sunlight beat down on the assembled workforce. The scientists began to walk across the well-maintained grass to the hole, prodding the earth with rods, testing for a mirage. Standing by the seventeenth in the glorious sunlight stood a seven-foot tall masked giant. The mask was of an old man's face. He wore gloves, a long dark trench coat and a trilby. He would have been hard to miss, if anyone could see him, for underneath his trench coat he wore a dark grey jumpsuit with a raised hexagonal pattern. The giant moved slowly and purposefully through the assembled mass towards the driving range, carefully navigating the scientists, soldiers and military police who were staring transfixed at the missing crater and although no one could see him, he was careful not to touch a soul.

Several hours later, another large man walked across the golf course in a jumpsuit. Hal was curious about the origin of the suit and how he discovered it. He ducked through the hedges and bracken at the edge of the rough and approached the crater in full invisibility, but there was no crater to be seen.

The seventeenth hole was immaculate, the finest groundsman's creation. Surrounding it were men in white coats and military personnel pulling out. Hal listened in on a conversation between two scientists:

"The fog and the crater's disappearance can't be a coincidence."

"Nothing else found?" replied the colleague.

"Zero debris, no unidentified metals, just the remnants of a vodka bottle and a set of tracks leading to the centre and back. Approximately size ten shoes."

Good guess Hal thought. He was actually a 9½ but had always found it difficult to purchase footwear due to his wide paddle feet.

"As for what was there..." the scientist trailed off, "your guess is as good as mine. Just pray it was… nothing bad."

Hal stood amongst the confused scientists with an incredible feeling of freedom, knowing that he was wearing the only evidence of the invisibility suit ever existing. As the sunlight beat down on him, he wanted to laugh, he wanted to smoke a cigarette and felt a strong sense that a belch was timely too. He chided himself for the previous day's lack of ambition and embarked on his own version of London Open House.

12 noon Invisibility ON.

13:00   Strolls down the centre of the Mall. Recalls the Michael Fagan incident of 1982.

13:20   Arrives at Buckingham Palace gates. Briefly entertains climbing the drainpipe, Fagan style, before walking past the guards.

13:27   Bypasses corgis, helps himself to a cheeseboard, sinks several large glasses of Chateauneuf du Pape, three bowls of olives and some Iberico Ham; a feast of kings.

14:05   Falls asleep on the throne. Not for the first time.

14:40   Discovers Her Majesty the Queen and Prince Philip are not in residence.

14:46   Eases disappointment by helping himself to a HRH lighter and matching loo roll. Visualises the creation of the Shed of Kings.

15:00   Waits outside Downing Street next to two armed policewomen. Follows the stern Minister for Education inside. The word 'egregious' comes to mind, he doesn't know what it means.

15:23   Stifles yawn within the Prime Minister's meeting. Feels a vast 'ham burp' rising to the surface, manages to supress it.

15:27   Intervention: squeezes the Prime Minister's knee, leaving one visible suspect; the Minister for Education. The Prime Minister furrows his brow tensely to facilitate a brief pause in his rhetoric. Then the happily married Prime Minister discretely reaches beneath the table to grab the Minister for Education's knee, giving it a little squeeze and the Minister a coy glance.

15:27–15:28   'Ha, I knew it,' Hal thinks. 'They're all at it.' Is about to leave when he looks at the party whip across the table. A second word pops into his head: 'oleaginous'.

15:29   Wonders what dictionary he swallowed that morning.

16:04   Leans against the clock mechanism inside Big Ben. Feels the call of nature and urinates in a dark corner. Considers his boundless freedom and wonders why he's urinating in Big Ben, when he could have in Downing Street.

16:22   Thinks about all of the banks he could rob but has no need for money. The redundancy he'd accrued from twenty-five years of long service as a telecoms engineer meant he never needed to work, ever.

17:55   Relocates to BBC Television Centre for the News at Six. Sits next to his favourite news anchor. Is amazed to discover the background is in fact a giant projection and the room smaller than he'd anticipated. Plays out the entire relationship in his mind as she reads an item about the presidential elections in a tight pencil skirt. Wonders what she would say if she knew he was there. Wonders if she would even see him.

18:01   Decides it would not work out.

21:30   Sits in the centre circle under the floodlights after the match at Loftus Road. As the supporters slowly file out, realises that sometimes you never feel as alone as when you're surrounded by other people.

22:15   Strolls down Regents Canal considering if there is anything worth returning home to. Looks at the large nets at the back of the Zoo. Wonders if the people in the wealthy cream mansion houses opposite are really happy. Considers a visit and evaluation.

22:16   Walks past the lights, colour and goths along Walkers Quay. The sky is overcast, cumulus clouds gang together in the East. Feels strangely sad.

With the beauty of Regents Park long gone, the towpath became darker, dirtier and more industrial, but invisibility had its privileges. Hal sat on a high wall overlooking the murky water. He was tired. It was a lot of walking in one day. Time for a cigarette.

On the towpath below, a homeless man slowly wheeled a shopping trolley containing all his worldly possessions. The wheels squeaked as he pushed it along, heavily stacked with clothing and items, but, over the pile, the man caught sight of two youths in their mid-twenties striding towards him. The youths altered their path to bring themselves on a collision course. The homeless man shifted direction then halted when the youths held their arms outstretched like a greeting.

"What you saying grandpa?" asked one of the youths enthusiastically.

"Yes, thank you," evaded the homeless man timidly trying to move on, his trolley wheel jammed in the uneven towpath brickwork.

"Yes what?" the shorter youth interjected. His name was

Raymond Trevena, his taller 'friend', Jason Cross or Jay.

"What's your name?" Jay growled. The homeless man tried to trundle on but his path was blocked. "I said, what's your name? Where you think you're going then eh?" Jay added, moving well within his personal space.

"I am but a homeless man, please."

"I said, what's your name?"

"Osiris."

"O-what?"

"Osiris."

"Where's that from?"

"Nairobi."

Raymond began to sniff all around the homeless man. "Jesus you stink," he said with contempt from every fibre of his body.

"God, you do really stink don't you?" added Raymond.

Osiris looked at the floor with sad eyes.

"You need a wash mate."

"Most definitely," said Raymond.

"Please, let me go," Osiris replied, but he was not allowed to finish his sentence. Jay struck him viciously with a blackjack on the arms and legs.

Osiris collapsed: "Please, no!"

"What business you got here anyway?"

"Think it's alright you being here, beggin'? This is our country." Jay dragged him up and punched him in the stomach with such force that both his feet left the ground. He yelped like a stricken fox.

"Come on then!" Raymond shouted, a shower of spittle engulfing Osiris's face. Hal felt sick. He pressed the lapel to materialise and ran into the nearby street. An unmarked police car drove towards him with its siren wailing. He held out his arm in a desperate attempt to flag it down but the car roared past, the siren lowering in pitch as it hurtled further and further into the distance. The street was deserted. A fox rummaged through an empty fast-food box by a parked car.

He gulped and cupped his face in his hands in indecision, wheezing as he jogged towards the colour and stalls of the main Camden strip: "Anybody?" he shouted. It would take ages to get there, to find someone. In the distance, he heard another yelp from the canal. Hal stopped in his tracks, looked deep into the honeycomb fabric of the suit and pressed the lapel button purposefully.

"I can't swim!" Osiris repeated, his eyes, red and tearful. Jay had grabbed him by the neck, holding him perilously on the edge of the dark, dirty canal.

"Dude, be quick!" said Raymond looking back and forth along the towpath for witnesses. "Hurry man." Suddenly he heard a voice from right in front of him.

"Too late!"

Raymond's hooded top flew over his head as it snapped back from an invisible strike dispatching him into the dark polluted canal with a splash. "Jay! Jay!" he screamed as he thrashed through the water, blood streaming from his nose. Jay's eyes were wide with panic and confusion before he felt a sudden blow to the stomach, instantly winding him. He fell back onto the concrete towpath. Osiris looked around in all directions, cowering.

Jay looked wildly in every direction, as if evading an angry wasp, his breath fast, hyperventilating, but the towpath was clear. He gasped as a large weight bore down on his chest, pinning him to the damp concrete.

"Get it off me!" he whined as he felt a hand around his neck. Then he heard the voice out of thin air: "I don't want to catch you again. Do we have an understanding?"

Raymond, who had just managed to clamber back onto the towpath, looked back at his friend pinned to the floor, then quickly surveyed all around him.

"Help!" Jay called out, seeing his water-sodden accomplice in the distance.

Raymond stopped, took one look at his friend pinioned by an unseen force and ran as fast as his low-slung jeans would allow.

"You bast…" Jay angrily squealed, but the pressure on his neck silenced him again. "Please no, w-what are you?"

Hal relaxed his pint hand, the adrenaline coursing through him. He didn't expect questions. This was a time of action. He knew only one thing: he needed something badass to say, something that would put the fear into the punk he was sat on. He glanced around at Osiris and then at the towpath wall covered in tags, fly posters for gigs and Anderson's Travelling Funfair. As he looked along the wall, he paused on a small yellow poster for Archway Church service. Taking a deep breath, he tried to recall every Charlton Heston movie he had ever seen and slowly, with gravitas, he said:

"I am The Holy Ghost."

He released his vice-like beer grip leaving Jay gasping for breath rolling across the concrete. Jay stumbled to his feet. Terrified and unsure of the invisible force, he fled along the dimly lit towpath as best he could. One arm held his neck, the other waved around in thin air in an attempt to fend off the unseen.

Hal couldn't remember the last fight he'd been in, but he felt totally alive, shaking, laughing. He reached across and grabbed Osiris by the lapels of his ripped coat staring into the depths of his large, sorrowful eyes.

"Still with me pal?" Hal asked, but Osiris looked through him. His weakened hands made an attempt to touch the invisible force, but just as he got closer to Hal he stopped and with his remaining strength moved his heels together then his knees. He arched his back, in prayer: "Thank you so much Lord, thank you. I am just a poor homeless man, Lord. I am but a poor homeless man and yet you touch me..."

"What are you doing?" Hal rapped him on the head.

"You touch me, then hit me. I am so unclean Lord, so unclean."

"You're Osiris right?"

"Yes, yes I am. You know my name. You know my name! Yes, Osiris from Nairobi, father of five. I am sorry to separate from my wife Lord, we fell out of love..."

"Listen, I am not the... oh, you fell out of love too? Look, I am not him upstairs or any part of the Trinity. I am not God. I don't even believe in that stuff okay? I just wanted to say something to scare those youths away." Osiris looked into thin air towards the origin of the voice then bowed again.

"Here," Hal said, his invisible index finger hovering over the lapel button. He found himself wavering. He looked at Osiris. Although hurt, somehow he was now defiant, his large red eyes, full of hope.

"Thank you, Lord. Thank you so much." From the horizon

in the East, a distant and deep crack of thunder rumbled. Hal turned towards the storm, the sky lit up with lightning strikes.

"It is you!" Osiris slowly repeated, his eyes wide.

"No, no it's this..." Forgetting he was still invisible, Hal pointed to the button on his lapel, then he looked at the blood on Osiris bowed before him. "Can you make it to a hospital?"

"I will make it my Lord. I am certain."

Hal looked back at the wall once again, at the small church poster and nearby flyer for the latest superhero movie and he wondered.

PART TWO

In a rain-soaked side-street in Bloomsbury, the heavy cycle-chain of a single-speed racer was being un-prised by a skilled thief. The chain was carefully re-attached to the post. The thief checked in all directions for eye-witnesses, slipped on his shoulder bag of tools and pushed the pedal down. After three revolutions, the bike came to a violent halt, hurling him high over the drop handlebars. "Arrgh!" he cried as he struck the hard, cobbled walkway. Amidst confusion and shock, he turned back to see the racer slowly right itself, wheel back to the railings and lock itself secure. Terrified, he fled into the night. The sky let out a distant rumble of thunder.

The top deck of the 242 bus was hot and clammy but relatively empty. At the back, three intimidating youths sat playing trance music from their mobile phone, nodding, frowning. The repetitive beat cut through the top deck annoying all within earshot. An elderly pensioner swivelled in his seat to look back at them. The youths stared right at him and as they did they slowly turned the volume up, making the old man wince. The youths cackled with laughter. A young mother turned in her seat to face them: "Do you mind turning it down please?"

"Eh?" replied the loudest of the group.

"The music, can you turn it down? People don't wanna hear your music."

"Mind your business, Miss."

"Can you turn it down?"

"So what's this gotta do with you? Does this have anythin' to do with you? Does this have anythin' to do with you?"

"It's not your room, it's a bus."

"It's my bus." The youths laughed but suddenly the phone flew out of his hand, levitating in mid-air just two feet in front of him, the music still playing.

"What's going on man?" The youth tried to grab it but it hovered out of reach.

"Obeah!" added another.

The phone hovered momentarily longer then hurled itself out of the open window.

"No! I ain't got insurance man." The youths raced off the bus, hitting the emergency door open button. The old man looked at the young mother.

"I didn't do that," she said.

In the distance, thunder rumbled again.

On the edge of the roof of a Broadgate financial building stood Michael Willis.

"Don't take another step!" he shouted, his eyes rolling within his gaunt face. Fifty feet of concrete roof lay in between him and Sally, the police mediator, and a further three hundred to the street.

"Michael, I just want you to know that there are people who love you, people that care. I know what happened was a terrible thing, an unfortunate thing, but we can help you."

"Shut up! Stay back. These are just words..."

"That's not true, Michael," Sally intervened.

"You make me sick." Michael was tearful, the amalgamation of medication, alcohol and drugs coursed through his spindly frame. The mediator rose to her feet; a mistake. Michael's head shook violently: 'No.' He took one look back into the eyes of the mediator, then at the street below and launched himself from the roof.

As he began his descent into the abyss, Michael found himself frozen but not falling. His arms flailed and his feet dangled towards the streets below, but an unseen force held the back of his jacket.

"Let go of me!" he screamed, but there was nobody holding onto him.

As the mediator and police darted across the roof towards him, Michael heard a voice whisper: "It's not your time yet. You must fulfil your purpose."

"What? What is this? Who are you?" He felt a stern yank pull him back onto the roof just as the equally confused police force surrounded him.

"It's alright son, it's alright," said an officer. There was a silent, unsaid understanding amongst the officers of the supernatural event they had all witnessed.

"My purpose," whispered Michael to the officers. "What is it?"

A few floors below, Hal materialised smiling in the sanctuary of the office stationery cupboard, the one place in every office that should have CCTV, but never does. "You must fulfil your purpose," he laughed, "now that was good." He reached over to a newly delivered metal filing cabinet still covered in plastic film. He began to heave, but found it easy to pick up with one hand. He put it down and flexed his minimal biceps, concealed in years of congealed lager fat. "Added strength? What other secrets do you hold?" He stroked the hexagonal honeycomb patterned fabric of the suit.

The remainder of Hal's night became a crime-fighting montage worthy of Jack Kirby. By 3am in the heavy rain, the outline of a figure ascended the final few levels of scaffolding and stood atop the Shard. He was a lion over his domain, the king of all he surveyed. In his deepest primal voice, Hal screamed: "I am!" Thunder rumbled, lightning streaked across the skyline, no one heard.

The following morning, Hal woke up with minor memory loss. Small gaps from the night before. He looked down to find himself still in the suit. Ordinarily this level of extensive wear would make anything smell, but the suit always smelt new. He immediately touched the lapel and once reassured by his temporal invisibility, released the button. Hal felt the aches and strains of exercise, a pastime which he had no time for, and edged across the damp garden path towards the house. Darcy, his neighbour's fourteen-year-old daughter, looked over the wooden fence into the Maybury garden. She stared, blowing bubble-gum until it popped.

"Holidays?" Hal asked, willing her to go play elsewhere.

Darcy shook her head. "You tired?"

"No," Hal replied at the patio door.

"You look tired."

"Thank you."

"Had a late night?" Darcy paused for effect: "Again?"

Hal felt a sudden inner-shiver. He looked at Darcy then his eyes traced up to her bedroom window. The ledge where Darcy smoked every night, which overlooked the Maybury back garden. He imagined a large dotted line being drawn from Darcy's ledge to the shed.

"See you around," Hal said wearily entering the house.

"See you around Mr Maybury."

The draught cutting through the Maybury kitchen indicated the front door was open. A loud bleep of a reversing truck could also be heard. Hal followed the bleeping noise through to the front to reveal Trina wearing an immaculate outfit, signing for a consignment from a delivery driver.

"Hi?" Hal said forcing out the words uncertain of whether a reception would be forthcoming.

"Hi," Trina pressed sharply through thin lips. He knew right there and then, this was going to be an economic exchange at best.

"How was Magda's?"

"What do you care?" She had a point; he really didn't care for Magda.

"What's the delivery?"

"Plates, crockery."

"We have plates."

"Well now we have more."

"What do we need more plates for?"

"The Renaissance Society meeting. I told you about it, didn't you listen?"

"What those witch..." Trina shot him a look but Hal corrected himself: "Which night did you say?"

"Thursday. I don't expect to see you around here after six, we clear? You're good at disappearing, disappear." Taking in the smallest box and leaving the others, Trina departed for the kitchen. Hal stood amongst the exquisitely designed delivery boxes in the hallway. On each one read: 'Fine Bone China'. He mouthed the words in disbelief and felt sick, it was a joint account, but his redundancy money. "Jesus H Trina, what's wrong with Ikea?"

In the street out front, the delivery driver sat with the sliding door open playing REO Speedwagon as he completed some paperwork. Hal bounded across the garden towards the van.

"Excuse me, how much did that lot cost?" The driver carefully removed a carbon copy receipt and handed it to Hal.

"You are kidding me?"

"Nope."

"I could have bought a car for that!"

"Cars," The delivery driver sighed, leaning closer. "Listen mate, it's your lucky day. We are giving a special thirty percent discount to all customers because of..." The driver winked at Hal, then glanced up into the sky and whistled. Hal looked on. "You know?" repeated the driver winking again and whistling at the sky before looking back at his befuddled customer, but the hint was unappreciated.

"You better turn on your TV pal." The delivery door slid shut and the driver was away, leaving Hal coughing in a cloud of exhaust fumes.

Within the forest of crockery boxes. Hal fired up the set and sat in his favourite chair. The old cathode ray set was taking an unusually long time to start up and Trina, expecting a row about the cost of fine dining, was surprised to see Hal's attention focused solely on the television. Finally a picture: outside St Barts Hospital a dignified lady in her sixties stood with the on-screen caption 'Mary Willis'.

"I don't know," she said to the gathering of assorted press, "I have seen the footage twenty times already, it's a miracle. Something saved my Michael, something brought him back." Tears streamed down her face as an aide hugged her. The press interjected with a barrage of questions and camera flashes.

"That is all," said her aide and led her away. The newscaster continued with an item about the banking crisis.

Hal switched channels: "There are reports of unexplained phenomena." He switched again: 'The Ten Commandments', classic Heston. Hal switched channels: "It's definitely some kind of media stunt, absolutely a viral marketing campaign with a religious bent. It might even be art."

"You mean an installation?"

"Of sorts."

"Do you not find it strange no one has come forward?"

"Once it reaches critical mass, we'll find out there's a new yogurt or movie or I dunno something. I actually find it in bad taste. Are we still in silly season? Is there no real news happening in the world?"

Hal switched again: music channel interview with a Californian pop starlet: "I'd love to go out for dinner with him, we'd just talk you know."

"Think him upstairs eats… dinner?" replied the presenter.

"You know what, he's probably sustained by pure energy or something; okay, I'd do the eating."

Channel three: a cheap, brightly coloured daytime TV debate. The studio camera panned across a Sikh, a rabbi, a priest and a Muslim cleric, and even more slowly onto the final guest, the homeless man from the towpath.

"Osiris?" Hal said aloud, leaning forward in his chair to get a better look.

"So tell me, what happened next?" asked the chiselled plastic presenter as earnestly as he could.

"Well, then He used his forces on the assailants: 'It is God that avengeth me, and subdueth the people under me, he delivereth me from my enemies.' Psalm 18:47-48."

"Psalm 18:47-48?"

"King James edition," nodded Osiris.

"And in light of yesterday's events, this morning both assailants Raymond Trevena and Jason Cross from East Ham have in fact turned themselves in and are being charged in Highbury Magistrates Court."

"There is no safe place from He."

"So, what did He do?" said the presenter catching the eye of the floor manager counting down.

"He brought the tempest, the rains last night."

The religious spokesmen shuffled uncomfortably in their seats. The presenter continued: "And then?"

Osiris reflected, deep in thought for a little while. "Well," he said, looking the presenter in the eye before pausing again for a long time: "Then he asked me for a cigarette."

Trina tutted. Uproarious laughter spread through the religious spokespeople, TV presenters and television crew. Everyone except Osiris, who stared dead into camera slowly, purposefully with his large red eyes: "You better watch your backs. He is coming for your asses, The Holy Ghost is regulating out there."

The presenter quickly interjected: "We would like to take the opportunity to apologise for the bad language, unfortunately this is live TV. We're very sorry for any offence."

Osiris pushed in front of the presenter and two security guards quickly burst into the TV frame to seize him: "The regulation has begun!" Osiris repeated. Chaos broke out in the studio.

"Szemét!" Trina shouted at the screen in disgust. "Micisoda egy szemét!" She walked to the door but had a sudden second thought: "I almost wish it was true. You would have a lot to be scared for."

Hal looked at her piercing eyes blazing. "You think?" he replied, transfixed by the screen. He turned to Trina "Can we...?" she slammed the kitchen door. "Talk...."

The Booze and Mags convenience store had remained unchanged in over twenty years. Mr Singh, the proprietor, caught sight of his most frequent customer and beamed,

"Hal Maybury. Good to see ya baby," he said with his perfectly aligned incisors reflecting the fluorescents at magnitude. Mr Singh called everybody baby, but on this day Hal looked particularly lost.

"I'm okay Mr Singh could I have...?"

"Twenty Lucky Strike?" Mr Singh interrupted. "Certainly

Hal baby. A little lubrication for you as well, or too early?" Hal looked at the booze rack and declined. As Mr Singh reached for a cigarette packet, Hal took in the large SLR camera and unusually large telephoto lens hanging from his neck, making Mr Singh look like a professional paparazzi not convenience store owner.

"You're into photography?" asked Hal.

"It takes all sorts of people to make a world." Mr Singh lifted a newspaper from the counter enabling Hal to read the headline:

'£50,000 reward for a picture of The Holy Ghost'

Beneath it, an artist's impression of a bearded spectral entity.

"Jesus H, in one night?" Hal mouthed in disbelief looking at the front page.

"Ah-ah-ah, blasphemy," replied Mr Singh. "You never know where He is but He's been very busy, very busy. Now look at that there." Mr Singh patted the newspaper. "Fifty thousand big ones baby! Yahoo! One minute, an MP is in a vice ring, the next, Second Coming. How you figure that?" Hal was unexcited, ashen. "You look like you have seen the He. Have you seen him Hal? We can split it?" Mr Singh half-joked. Hal walked to the exit. "What you up to today?"

"I gotta re-fortify the shed."

"A man's shed is his castle baby." On the counter sat the box of cigarettes Hal had left behind.

The owner of the Spy Shop by East Finchley station was wide, a 4:3 body trapped in a 16:9 universe. "How fortified?" he replied, his voice sombre. Hal reached into his pocket and pulled out an Agamemnon Kebabs napkin with a hand-drawn schematic diagram in biro. He slid it across the glass counter. The owner rested his designer glasses on the bridge of his nose, inspecting the plan, nodding in agreement. He reached under the table and placed a small plastic device on the glass counter. In the centre of the device was a neon thumb icon. The owner looked at the thumbprint and Hal moved his thumb onto it. The device bleeped in approval and the owner fixed Hal a thoughtful glance.

"How soon can it be done?" Hal asked.

"How soon do you need it done?" replied the owner, clicking his knuckles.

The workers at Anderson's Travelling Funfair had all but finished packing up on the heath, ready for the show to move on. Their cavalcade of nearly roadworthy vehicles had begun to assemble, but as the crews de-rigged, a giant figure wearing the mask of an old man moved unseen by all. A bull terrier chained to a wooden stake began to bark. He turned to stare at it. Immediately, the terrier reverted from barking to furious howls of distress, whining sharply, as if injured. "What's wrong Bullseye, eh girl? Bullseye?" The tattooed ride attendant attempted to placate the animal; however, the invisible intruder had turned his attention onto something else.

Inside the Hall of Mirrors, the giant man cast no reflection, stooping to avoid the ceiling. He pressed the button on the lapel of his jumpsuit and materialised. With his long arms he reached towards the floor and picked up the stub of a crushed cigarette. The ride attendant wandered in, startled:

"We're closed mate. Park's closed."

Ignoring him, the giant continued to examine the cigarette closely.

"Come along mate, move it. Come on, you ain't supposed to be here," the attendant said raising his voice.

Slowly and deliberately the masked giant looked up and turned to face the ride attendant who immediately began to backtrack for, as he looked at the masked man's face, the attendant realised that he had no eyes, just holes where the eye sockets should have been. Alarmingly, he was able to see straight through to the back of the mask. There was no head in between.

"Easy fella," the attendant said stepping back.

"I am not supposed to be here," replied the giant. It was a statement, not a question.

After the media furore of day one, Hal took a moment for reflection sat on top of the Art-Deco Southgate Tube Station. Whilst invisible, he considered the pros and cons of the superhero business, but he already found it too exhilarating and made a decision. On that night and the one after, Hal hit the streets, regulating.

There was an immediate and marked decrease in street crime numbers. The Metropolitan Police commissioner was conducting a formal investigation without any leads. Hal knew all about this as he would sit in on their investigative meetings and brainstorms, although the official line was 'things were positive'. The newspaper ransom swiftly increased to £75,000 and then £100,000. There were reports of a glamour model wearing only lingerie tying herself to her bed and on hunger strike until The Holy Ghost would take her. Hal briefly entertained the thought, even considered the ethics of infidelity whilst invisible. She was subsequently sectioned.

The non-believing, vice-filled Hal struggled with the concept of impersonating an Almighty God, but was also aware he possessed an acutely natural talent for the role. His 'Heston' impersonation was near-pitch perfect. He'd boned up on bible passages and the extra strength gleaned from the suit enabled him both to smoke and drink whilst on patrol, but it was tiring. He had to walk or get public transport everywhere as a car driven by an invisible driver would undoubtedly attract attention, apart from on the Bishops Avenue where everybody just looked at the vast houses. And although his suit could render him invisible irrespective of the time of day, Hal's time, his favourite time, was the night.

In the early mornings, checking his neighbour's ledge for the ever-watchful, bubble-gum-chewing Darcy, Hal would return to his shed. It had seen a few changes since its customisation by the Spy Shop. The windows were one way. Entry was via thumbprint and what appeared to be an ordinary suburban shed on the outside was a technological fortress on the inside.

Hal surveyed the city from five monitors. He knew he could only look at one at any one time, but Hal liked his setup flamboyant like that. From a specially lit rail hung his favourite item, the suit. Next to that, an especially elevated fridge of beer and a cigarette rack. Hal activated the thumbprint alarm system, and fell asleep in the garden gazebo. When he awoke, he found himself staring at the light-polluted London sky. These were the best of days he thought, the salad days. It was time again to patrol and the fourth night since he first uttered the words: "I am The Holy Ghost."

In a large and desolate area of Camberwell grassland three men smoked in the darkness. Occasionally a passer-by would approach them, money would exchange hands and the passer-by leave. Hal studied the group from the scrub behind, stubbing out his cigarette, careful to remain downwind of the trio. He pressed the lapel button and invisibly and silently approached through the long grass. As he closed in, he was able to hear the men talking, but not what was said. The group stood in the darkness with their backs to him. Hal moved to within twenty feet, then fifteen, when he felt a light pulling sensation around his ankle. He looked down to see a thin piece of fishing wire dragged by his leg. On pulling the wire, a small bell rang in the darkness.

The men immediately turned, looking directly at Hal but not with their eyes. Each man had a set of thermal imaging goggles strapped to his face. Hal began to back away in a zigzag but the men tracked his movements, left and right, up and down; the thermal imaging picking up Hal's head and hands, no torso. Hal backed off, tripping another wire which made a different small bell ring. One of the men slowly began to move into a flanking position. The tallest and meanest-looking of the three men was wiry with long hair. "Come here," he hissed, beckoning with his finger. "Come here…."

The men pressed the buttons on their goggles to alternate between thermal vision and normal. The outline of Hal was visible only in thermal mode. "Told you he was just a man," laughed the leader. In unison they each extended a small telescopic baton. Although the suit provided enhanced strength, these men were strong, organised and in their prime. For the first time in days Hal thought of 'The Decline' and his own activities.

"Be gone men of evil," he boomed, but the gang edged closer, in a triangle formation.

Another bell rang. Hal looked to his feet but there was no trip wire this time. From his peripheral vision, he saw a shape in the gloom. A fourth man rushing in. He didn't see the punch coming. A vicious strike from the side sent him crashing to his knees, his world spinning. The men stood over Hal, snarling, laughing. Hal tried to crawl away. The leader swung his boot into his abdomen. Hal howled in agony.

"No! Stop!" he cried. He started to crawl but one of the gang stood on his hand.

"My daddy told me never to believe in ghosts, you know that? Where you going? Where you going eh?"

The leader pulled out a shiv and swung it in towards Hal's chest. Hal tried to block. The shiv slid under the sleeve of the suit and into his arm. Blood spurted out of the sleeve into the night and the men set upon him with a flurry of kicks and batons. Hal lay in the grass, beaten, wheezing and bloody. The leader stood over him looking down triumphantly in his thermal goggles. From inside his long leather coat he slid out a silenced-pistol and slowly raised it to Hal's chest.

"Finish him," said one of the others.

"It's nothing personal," said the leader. "I just think you'd be better off in the afterlife."

Hal looked weakly into the thermal imaging lenses covering the man's eyes. He gasped with short rasps of breath.

"You know something, I don't even care about the reward," the leader growled then laughed, his shadow falling across Hal in the grass.

"Please, no," Hal pleaded, but could only manage a whisper: "Please."

The leader coldly and calmly cocked the pistol, staring into Hal's eyes the whole time. Hal looked on, blinking slowly, imagining what could have been, wondering if anyone would find his body, when he felt an unusual surge of mental alertness and an overriding urge to look at his chest. Very slowly, he raised his head and looked down his torso. Even in the dark, he noticed it. In the middle of the suit, dead centre, was a second button. Instinctively, he raised his bloody arm and pressed it. A small shockwave of energy hurled Hal's arms out to his side.

As he stood over the body, something caught the gang leader's attention. Small lines of light began spreading across the hexagonal honeycomb lines of the suit. The honeycombs spread up from the neck, quickly growing up and over his face until the suit completely covered him from head to toe.

"I am going to count to three," the wiry leader said before

immediately emptying the silenced magazine into Hal's prone body. There was no movement, but a low hum of power from the suit, a hum that gradually became louder and louder. The suit glowed red then a brilliant, intense white. A white so bright that everything within thirty metres was illuminated as if it was daytime. Then its brightness increased to the magnitude of a star. The gang screamed, engulfed in the whiteout.

Seconds later the honeycomb structure retreated from Hal's face. His body lay motionless, eyes closed. All around him, the men shouted in agony, incoherent: "I can't see! I can't see!" screamed the leader.

"I can't see," said another.

Their faces and hands were red raw and burnt.

"Help me!" The third man cupped his hands over his face writhing around on the floor, slowly Hal's eyes opened. He was alive! In a haze, he surveyed the scene. The gang members screamed and bawled, clawing at their eyes, their thermal goggles long discarded in the disorder. Hal was unable to comprehend that he was even alive or what fate had befallen the men. Invisibility was OFF and the central chest button in the suit had disappeared.

Slumped on the grass, Hal reached for the lapel button and pressed it repeatedly, but the suit was unresponsive. He was unable to become invisible. A gang member stumbled towards him, grasping at the air in panic. Hal pushed his arm away, avoiding the mass of outstretched arms and limbs of the others. He managed to rise to his feet and, as he did, amidst the chaos and calls, he became aware of the extent of his injuries. The leader was close, breathing hard on his knees. Hal raised his boot to kick him when the leader shouted; "Who's there? Who's there?"

Hal stood over him, watching him furiously claw at his eyes and burnt face, filled with thoughts of vengeance, but an agonising pain overrode him. He looked on as the men scrabbled around and turned away, trudging slowly across the scrubland. Light glinted off an alarm wire. Hal changed course to drag his leg through it. A bell rang again and the disorientated quartet screamed. Fleetingly, he smiled then grimaced as he looked at his hands, covered in blood.

Hal made his way across the grass as best he could, moving as far away from the gang as possible. Their screams echoed in the distance, but he found the direction of the screams soon scattered across his senses and the street lamps ahead became a phantasmagoria of light, the horizon warping. The only constant was the sound of his footsteps and the sour taste of blood in his mouth.

"Thank you," he whispered to the suit as he continued towards the hazy street lamps. "Thank you."

A black shape lay ahead in the grassland. As he got closer it was clear the shape was in fact the carcass of a dead dog. Hal trod straight through it without the energy to walk around, the stench temporarily returning him to the land of the living. Several steps further, he reached concrete. The South London street was empty. From behind him he heard the sound of an approaching car engine. Hal turned and tried to lift his arm. The driver slowed, rolled down the window shouting: "Junkie scum!" before screeching away. The temporal light of hope in Hal's eyes disappeared. Then, just a little further ahead, he saw a bus stop. He staggered towards it, concentrating all his energy on every step, first thirty metres, then twenty-five. As he approached, he was able to read the electronic timetable displaying 'Due' for several buses. Hal stumbled, step by step, closer and closer. "Almost there," he said, but the red writing of the arrivals indicator became gradually darker until his whole world faded to black.

As he looked around at the intense whiteness surrounding him, he considered that Heaven was exactly as he would have imagined it to be, if he had believed in it. It was a brilliant white, mysterious and magnificent, and Hal felt free as if he was floating. He even let out a sound, "Pah." He didn't know why. The brightness dissipated and a room came into view. Hal inhaled the sterile scent of cleanliness with a momentary sense of disappointment and relief.

"Can you hear me?" a voice softly repeated. He turned his attention to the out-of-focus doctor standing over him.

"How did I get here?" Hal added, slowly fazing in and out of consciousness. Gingerly, he pulled himself upright to a seated position, grimacing the whole way.

"You're a very lucky man," added the doctor as he commenced his examination. "A dog walker found you unconscious by a bus stop. Follow my finger." The doctor moved his finger around in the air as Hal's eyes tracked his movements. The doctor began prodding him.

"Ow!" Hal barked, not amused.

"There's some bruising on the ribs. Feel any pain here?" the doctor asked, holding Hal's forearm.

"Ow! Jesus H Doc!"

"Do you have any recollection of what happened? You appear to have been attacked and..." The doctor kept talking but to Hal his voice trailed off as if reduced in volume by an imaginary remote control. Pulling back the thin hospital sheets revealed Hal was wearing a white hospital robe with colourful polka dots. The bleep of the heart-rate monitor next to the bed swiftly increased. Hal began to search his surroundings with a newfound urgency, groaning as he did.

"Please, Sir, can you relax?"

Ignoring the doctor, Hal opened the bedside cabinet.

"Where is she?" The heart-rate monitor continued to rapidly increase.

"What are you after?"

"Where is she!" Hal demanded. "Did you cut her up?"

"Sir, you need to rest."

"Did you cut her up?" The doctor looked on motionless. Hal let out a big gasp of air, defeated, staring into space: "You don't understand."

"You came here alone, Sir."

"It's the suit. I call it a her. I call it that." Hal was lost. The doctor scratched his forehead and then reached below the clipboard at the bottom of Hal's bed and at the bottom of the bed pulled out the suit. As soon as he saw it Hal's grey eyes came alive in childlike wonder. The doctor passed the suit across the hospital bed. Although it was covered in dirt and blood, somehow it was intact. Hal sighed and closed his eyes in relief.

"You're lucky, she wouldn't like that you know, being cut up," Hal ran his hands softly across the honeycomb exoskeleton, tenderly stoking the fabric with all the energy he was able to muster. He pulled the suit to his chest. Slowly, his heart-rate decreased.

"She wouldn't like that," Hal repeated, the haze returning. He looked at his bandaged arm. "What's the damage?"

"You've been attacked; the arm is okay, just bruising."

"What about the gunshots?"

"You weren't shot, were you? Where?"

Hal positioned the suit so he could see the chest. Combing his hand across it, he carefully removed three bullet casings trapped within its fibre. Raising his eyebrows in surprise, he smiled: "Bulletproof."

He slid over and pressed the lapel button. Invisibility ON. He pressed the button once again: Invisibility OFF. Hal laughed to himself then had a moment of realisation, raising his head he saw the astonished doctor looking at the suit and then at him. He pressed the lapel once button again. He could feel the doctor piecing together the entirety of his existence.

"Well look at that. Not what you thought I bet. Wife always told me I was sloppy."

"How long have you two been going out?" the doctor asked.

"A week or so, only seriously in the last few days. It's a new relationship."

Hal became distant again, then smiled: "The wife doesn't know."

"You're married?"

"Two whole years, about 172 days good, 200 days fair to middling and the rest." Hal paused: "Pah. She's not religious either." He stared into space.

"And you?"

"Before the redundancy you know, I used to be a telecoms engineer." Hal felt around for his keys: "You got a cigarette, Doc?" The doctor pointed to the no-smoking sign. "Guess that wasn't your question was it?"

"You know the police are outside. They would like to interview you about the assault. I can let them in if you would like."

"Gonna be a tough write-up, that one."

"Three men were also admitted this evening. All three apparently wanted criminals. All three had an assortment of second- and third-degree burns between ten and fifteen percent. They claim to have seen a bright light. They were discovered cowering together in an area of scrubland, not far from where you were found, holding onto each other, pleading for their lives. Several witnesses corroborate their testimony. The light was so bright there have been reports of sightings as far north as Potters Bar. All three men have extensive burning to their retinas, resulting in permanent loss of vision."

Hal stared straight ahead. "They're blind?"

"That's correct."

Hal's mind flashed back to being within the suit as it closed up to protect him and seeing the faint orange glow of light around him.

"They claim it was The Holy Ghost," the doctor continued. "They say he was just a man."

"Did they say anything else?"

"Not as yet."

Hal twisted his body to let his legs dangle off the side of the bed, grimacing as he did.

"Where do you think you're going?"

"I gotta check out, Doc."

"You can't go anywhere in your condition!"

"You're probably right." Hal paused before turning back to the doctor: "You know Doc, do you like TV?"

"What?"

"It's a simple question."

"Sometimes."

"I like TV. I have ninety days of TV listings at home. The wife calls it the idiot box. Guess that makes me an idiot; maybe she was right."

"You need to lie down. Rest, you may have a head trauma. We need to run more tests."

"I watched a documentary once. It was about medicine, young doctors and nurses, the hopes of the next medical generation, that kind of thing. None of them were in decline, at least not yet. Wasn't my bag I must say. No offence, Doc."

"None taken."

"I was just after some filler for the evening session of the snooker championships to kick off. Anyway, there was this part where all the young doctors were told about this oath, an ancient oath of good medical practice. Now what was that called, Doc?"

"You mean the Hippocratic Oath."

"The Hippocratic Oath, that's the one, good memory, I guess that's why you're a doctor." Hal looked the doctor in the eyes: "Now what was that phrase used, oh I remember, 'patient confidentiality', that's it isn't it?"

"Patient confidentiality," the doctor forced through pursed lips before sighing, a wry smile crept across his face. The suit slid up Hal's body by itself and Hal stood, shaky but strengthened by its inner power.

"You shouldn't leave."

"The Holy Ghost is getting a minicab, who'd have thought?"

"Hey, have you spoken to anyone you know about this?"

"Apart from her?" Hal looked at the suit, then shook his head.

"Maybe I should." Hal stood up opposite the doctor. "What's your name, Doc?"

"Christopher."

Hal extended his hand to shake. "Charlton," Hal replied. They shook hands then Hal pressed the lapel button and faded in opacity until he could no longer be seen. His footsteps led to the door, which appeared to open by itself.

"Thank you," Hal's voice said out of thin air. "Maybe I will talk to someone."

"Who?"

"No idea."

A police officer poked his head round the door, to a room containing an empty bed, a bemused doctor and no assault victim.

Hal stumbled through Triage towards the exit following the brightly coloured painted lines on the floor then changed his mind, wondering further into the hospital. A policeman stood guard outside a room. Hal bypassed him and entered. Inside the small ward lay his four assailants, each handcuffed to their metal beds. Each man's eyes and face were bandaged, with two of the men hooked up to breathing apparatus. Hal stood for a moment, watching the badly damaged men trying to breathe. He pulled up a chair next to the gang leader.

"Remember me?" Hal said in his normal voice. The leader's breathing quickened.

"Guess that's a yes."

Hal placed his hand on the leader's head; "Quite a bad situation, don't you think? You unable to see and me invisible."

The gang leader wheezed in panic. He reached across with his bandaged hand to hit the emergency button but Hal pushed it out of reach.

"Do you like hospitals? I never really cared for them myself, no, I really never did. Maybe it's the smell, what do you think?"

"W-what do you want?" the leader gurgled in agony. Hal smiled.

The press helicopter circled the South London scrubland at night. The green and black hues of night-vision revealed the scorched grass in a fifty-metre circle. In the middle of the circle was an untouched piece of grassland. The camerawoman gazed down in astonishment. She switched to her telephoto lens and turned to the pilot: "Hold it right there."

"What we got?"

The pilot manoeuvred the controls for the helicopter to hover. The camerawoman snapped off a few shots before switching to an ENG news camera to record everything. The pilot held position, without line of sight, frequently looking at the camerawoman to get a lead on the position. The camerawoman made an audible gasp.

"What?" asked the pilot.

The camerawoman picked up her mobile phone and hit speed dial.

"Jack."

"News desk, Holly is that you?"

"Hold pages 1, 2, 3, 4, 5 and 7."

"Is this this some kind of joke?"

"Do it Jack, do it now."

PART THREE

The Maybury's lounge was alive with the music of Mozart. The ornate grey oak table was laid as finely as a department store window. It was Thursday night, the night of the Renaissance Society's bi-monthly meeting. All the club members were female, in their late thirties to mid-forties and wore immaculate outfits, conveying to some extent the glow of wealth.

"Well, it's almost Cabernet day isn't it?" declared Constance, chairwoman of the division.

"Aha, yes," replied Evelyn.

"Trina, this is simply divine," added Angora amidst a chorus of: "Wonderful" and "Fabulous" and "She's done a wonderful job." However, Constance, appeared pensive. A hush quickly descended across the table, as when Constance was pensive the rest of the Renaissance Society were pensive by default. Their judgemental faces centred on Trina.

Constance broke the silence: "I have to admit, I was a little unsure of you in the beginning Trina." The ladies clung to her every word as she stared long and hard at Trina. "But, this has been a first-rate evening. You've really pulled it out. Don't you agree ladies?" The uncertainty around the table instantly transformed into rapturous approval: "Absolutely first rate."

"And where did you get this china? It's divine."

"It really is."

"And those kitten heels?"

Trina exhaled a long sigh of relief, beaming with pride. Finally, she'd made it.

Amidst the hubbub, the kitchen door slowly creaked open. A dishevelled Hal Maybury stood in the doorway. A second hush spread through the room leaving only the sound of Trina's Mozart CD playing softly in the background. Hal looked terrible: wounded, bruised and beaten.

"Evening ladies," Hal smiled, displaying blood-stained teeth. The Renaissance Society recoiled collectively in horror.

"What's happened to you? I thought I told you not to..." Trina bit her lip in fury.

"Long day dear," Hal followed Trina's eyes glaring at the small bottle of whisky in his hand. "Purely medicinal."

"Ghastly," whispered Angora to Evelyn. "Absolutely ghastly." Evelyn nodded in contempt.

"You've been fighting and drinking! Get out! Get out!" Trina shouted.

"Look, I am a little short of change, you have anything for Stelios the cabbie? Wanted to give him something extra."

"Tűnj el a házamból! Tűnj el a házamból!" Trina yelled repeatedly on an exponential upward curve of rage.

"I'll... be in the shed." Hal grimaced and trudged through the kitchen wincing with every step and grasping at a handful of canapés. On seeing Stephanie, from the female-only spa, he briefly paused.

"You know all that extra work you're putting in down the gym. It's really paying off."

"Why thank you, Hal," Stephanie blushed.

The ladies collectively shot Stephanie a dark look. Hal trudged across the dark gloom of the garden. In the lounge, tears streamed down Trina's cheeks.

"I am sorry, I am so sorry. He's an animal! Ez egy Állat!" she said, weeping into her aperitif. Constance at the head of the table, rose to her feet and set down a chair next to Trina. As Trina sobbed, Constance comforted her, placing a hand on her shoulder, and brushing the hair from her eyes.

"It's not always easy is it?" said Constance calmly. She looked around at the other members who instantly and in unison, tilted their heads in understanding.

"I've tried. I've really tried. He was not meant to be here."

"Trina. We can pray for you."

"Pray? We pray?" Trina added with great uncertainty. Constance nodded slowly.

"It might be a good idea," added Angora.

"Haven't you seen the TV?" Constance asked.

"I have but..."

"He's back. The Holy Ghost is back."

"Isn't that some kind of media stunt?"

"He's back and He could be anywhere," Angora interjected.

"At any time," added Constance. "And he's taking vengeance."

"He could even be right here now." Evelyn's eyes darted around the ceiling of the Maybury's dining room. "Seriously."

"You better get on the right team," Constance added looking

into Trina's tearful eyes. "It's okay." She cupped the back of Trina's head, stroking her hair: "It's okay. You just have to let Him in. He can help you. He can help your husband too."

"I'm not sure that this is me..." It was in this moment she recalled that this was perhaps her only shared value within her marital relationship. She surveyed the entire table, at the eyes upon her, at the weight of expectation, at her resolute failure to create the perfect dinner party. Somehow she found herself closing her eyes and slowly bowing her head.

Constance began to pray: "Our Father, please help Trina, please help her in this trying time. Give her strength and help her to hold her head up high. Our Father, please cast out the evil that her husband may yet commit and spare him from your wrath. Spare him for your wrath, for he does not know what he does. We know you have returned, Our Father, we have seen the signs. We know you walk amongst us again and we are your servants Lord. We, the members of the Finchley and Totteridge Renaissance Society, are ready to do thy bidding. We pray for you Trina, we pray for you, for we know the Lord has returned, The Holy Ghost is here, the hour of judgement is at hand. He is returneth Trina."

"He is returneth," replied the ladies in unison.

"He is returneth Trina."

"He is returneth," replied the ladies once again.

"He is returneth Trina." Trina was uncomfortable; however, around her the usually shark-like ladies of the Finchley and Totteridge Renaissance Society seemed unusually kind, maybe even optimistic.

"He... is... returneth," Trina slowly repeated. "He is returneth."

Hal stood on the lawn in the darkness, half way in between his house and the shed, not sure whether to walk forwards, backwards or lie down. He just stopped. His body ringing in widespread pain, feeling 'The Decline' more than ever before. As he stood, with his paunch overshadowing his feet, He popped another painkiller. From the other side of the fence he heard a match strike. Hal turned to see his neighbour's daughter, Darcy, standing on a box, her head peering into the Maybury Garden.

"Don't you understand the concept of private property?" groaned Hal.

Darcy blew smoke from her nose insouciantly.

"You shouldn't be doing that either."

"Doing what?"

"That." Hal jutted his chin out at Darcy's cigarette.

"You smoke."

"Following in my footsteps won't get you any place special."

"You do alright."

"What would your father say? Ever think about that?"

"He don't visit too much these days. It's just me and mum. She passed out a couple of hours ago on the sofa with a bottle of vodka. She'll come to soon I guess, she sleeps through, sometimes."

"She do that a lot?"

"Yeah."

"I have an uncle, somewhere in Manchester, don't know

whereabouts." Darcy disappeared behind the fence and reappeared with a fresh cigarette. She held it, arm outstretched, across the divide, smiling.,

"I can't," Hal whispered softly.

"You've given up?"

"It would be... unethical."

"But you bummed one from me last week."

"That was when I wasn't… it's a long story." Hal groaned, his face moving into a patch of light, revealing his injuries.

"You've been hurt," Darcy, looked concerned. "Who by?"

"Didn't have time to ask them."

Darcy looked at Hal sternly. "I hope you hurt them." A light came on downstairs in Darcy's house, followed by a crash and a deranged call of her name. It was her mother.

"She's come to. I better go. Have a nice night out."

"I am not going out," Hal protested into thin air, looking on as her small silhouette entered the lounge.

"Where have you been?" screamed Darcy's mother.

"The garden, Mum."

"Where have you been? I told you. What did I say about being out? You're just like your father."

From the garden, Hal heard a slap, followed by another.

"Mum!" Darcy's scream was followed by a flurry of slaps close together. Hal's tired hand slid across to the lapel button and pressed it, watching his feet become transparent. From the lounge of 13 Clifton Terrace the sounds of Darcy's mother ceased as swiftly as they had begun. A silhouette appeared in their patio window. Darcy's mother stood staring across the grass, lighting a cigarette.

"Jesus H," said Hal amidst the shadows of the shed. "Jesus H!"

He awoke dripping in sweat. A nightmare. He found himself rubbing the suit once again for reassurance. It was at least mid-morning and a Friday. Hal sat bolt upright in his favourite easy chair and checked his wounds. The bruises to his ribs and head were considerably less substantial, although he still looked like he'd been in a fight and lost. He deducted that the suit appeared to possess a regenerative ability. The TV was still on from the night before. On the 24-hour news channel, a continuous helicopter shot of Camberwell parkland. Immediately, he recognised it. A large crowd had congregated. In the centre of the grassland was a giant dark circle, almost 150 feet in diameter. Everything within the circle was charred: trees, park benches and trash. At the epicentre of the scorched circle was an area of untouched green grass and in that lay the imprint of Hal's body. His arms thrown to the side, his legs together. It was a uniquely unmistakable symbol. Hal's imprint looked like a green, rotund Holy Cross. Below it on the rolling ticker:

'New unexplained religious phenomena – Camberwell!'

The news anchor was in full-flow: "Four men were found at the scene, all blinded by a light. Their names were: Sam Kent, Aldus Rain, Leroy Carson and Karl 'Bumpy' Heig, and in news just in – the men have confessed to a string of over thirty major crimes, including two unsolved murders and have offered police full co-operation. When asked whether this unidentifiable Holy Ghost had any influence on this decision, the men had no comment but said they all felt a sudden compulsion. The Archbishop of Canterbury is currently visiting the site, hailed by locals as a shrine."

A series of vox-pops followed:

"I saw the light, no word of a lie, I saw it, I don't know what caused it but it weren't human."

"I was asleep actually, it woke me, felt like daytime, looked out across the grass and it was bright, exactly like a bright dome. As soon as I saw it I knew. I knew he was Him, you know, Him upstairs. Better get to church I guess."

"Either it's aliens or, well, I don't know what it is. Grass looks strange, ain't even seen grass like that and I've seen a lot of grass."

"Personally, I didn't believe in any of it."

"Those criminals saw the light, that's clear, it's clear."

"Beware of false prophets and people bearing false gifts, anything false really."

"Two unsolved murders?' said Hal. "Only told them I'd be watching them for the rest of their lives. Fancy that."

He channel hopped: "Flight BA939 from Dusseldorf has just made an emergency landing at Heathrow with trapped landing gear. All of the passengers aboard the flight survived without injury. An aviation expert has described it as a miracle."

In the arrivals terminal, a passenger screamed for joy: "Thank you so much, Holy Ghost. I love you! I love you!"

"Uh-oh," said Hal, staring into the screen.

He changed channel again: "There's been in-fighting between Catholics, Christians, Muslims and Pagans on the Old Kent Road with additional flash points in Stamford Hill and

Southall. The source of conflict is unknown but it is believed to be linked to the recent supernatural events. We're now joined by Professor Silva, Professor of Theology at Trinity College. Professor Silva, thank you for joining us. What's your view on this religious in-fighting?"

"Well, essentially, I believe the flashpoint on the Old Kent Road is in fact a microcosm of global concerns, but, essentially, it's a battle of monotheism. They all wish to lay claim to whom or what they perceive as the source of these mysterious events and it will continue and it will get worse."

"Do you believe there actually is a Holy Ghost? Is this a religious phenomenon or a supernatural one?"

"What's the difference? In the strictest sense of belonging to a specific religion, possibly not, but these phenomena of the last few days are still left unexplained."

"So you're keeping an open mind?"

"Well yes, I would say so." Professor Silva smiled a nervous smile.

"No," Hal groaned, looking at the footage.

He channel hopped. On St Thomas' Hospital and other prominent buildings, HG had been written in giant spray paint letters by a graffiti crew wearing face masks, hoodies and carrying stylish walking canes. The crew left an online video:

"We are the disciples. We roll with He. Don't cross us, or you'll end up on the cross."

"Oh no!" Hal said and swapped channel. Theology 101:. "Oh no!"

Hal channel hopped: "The Pontiff has yet to make a statement."

He channel hopped: "Several airlines have laid on special

charter flights to and from Lourdes to Camberwell, via Stansted. Flights to London, especially from the USA are completely sold out. We spoke to the Aviation Authority: 'This is normally the tail end of high season, there's been an unprecedented spike in scheduled and chartered flights. It's the busiest it's ever been. Whatever your beliefs or standpoint, the recent events have been spectacular for tourism.'"

"Oh God no," Hal sighed at the screen.

He channel hopped and saw a man outside Westbourne Park bus garage holding a sandwich board with 'The end is nigh' on it: "How long are you going to stand there?" asked the journalist.

"Till the end of next week."

"End of next week?"

"Yeah, we'll pretty much be in Ragnarok by then, give or take a day."

He channel hopped: Channel three. The same daytime show he'd watched a few days ago and once again Osiris was an interviewee, a picture of sartorial elegance: dressed head to toe in white; white blazer, white trousers, white slacks, white panama hat waistcoat and tie. No longer sharing the sofa alongside other religious spokespeople. Osiris was the main event.

"Jesus triple H!" gasped Hal. The plastic identikit presenter looked sombre as Osiris sat resplendent under the studio lights, next to his agent.

"What did I tell you? All of this would come to pass."

"Will there be more incidents? In your opinion?"

"Well as I have previously stated on this very network, his work has only just begun. I think it's very reasonable to presume that there will be much more of this to come."

"The regulation as you put it?"

"Indeed."

"Oh no there won't," Hal grunted, pressing the power button on the TV remote. Opting against encountering Trina's rage head-on, he stealthily closed the shed door, navigated to the back fence and clambered over it into the lane of garages. He stopped to glance back at the house, then kept moving. As he walked away the Maybury kitchen curtain was slowly pulled back. Trina watched unmoved, her face pressed against the glass. Slowly she closed her eyes and made the sign of the cross. "Én meg imádkozom érted. Szükséged van rá," she said softly.

The Finchley streets were unusually desolate for a Friday morning. Even the Booze and Mags convenience store was closed. The air was hot and sticky and a hot haze spread across the vanishing point of the road. In the window of one semi-detached house hung huge cloth Holy Cross hung, from another bellowed a CD of choral hymns. Hal nervously crossed the road. Up ahead, a group of young kids played tag in their driveway.

"I'll be The Holy Ghost," shouted a girl with a frying pan attached to her head.

"No, I'll be The Holy Ghost," the small boy said and pointed his hands: "Energy attack."

Seeing Hal, the boy redirected his 'attack' at the passer-by: "Pow-pow, energy attack, energy attack, energy attack, pow-pow biblical blindness!"

The eerie silence continued for street after street. The main roads were quiet, the side roads, quieter. In all his years in Finchley, Hal had never experienced anything like it. Invisibility was a non-requirement, nobody was around to see him anyway. In the distance the sound of people. As he gravitated in that general direction, he began to pass the occasional pedestrian: an elderly West Indian couple, then a trio of Polish construction workers. Gradually the streets became populated with uniform movement in the same direction towards the sound. Hal blended in amidst the steady stream of people.

The group turned the corner onto the main road. It was total roadblock: an assortment of stalls, vendors selling cheap vinyl prints of 'Holy Ghost' T-shirts, baseball caps, tote bags, flashing crosses, plastic 'Jesus Lives' rattles and shashlik kebabs. The unruly bazaar had vibrant colours, smells and music and, at the epicentre of the convergence, the local church gleamed in the sunshine. Hal was open mouthed.

As soon as the service ended, a mass of people streamed in through the main and side doors into the already packed church hall. Father O'Malley mopped his brow; with non-stop services day and night for the last few days, he was beat. His congregation had swelled exponentially to the point where he required volunteer stewards. All across the country and across faiths, there was a similar pattern.

Father O'Malley retired to his private room, a medium-sized ante chamber, took a seat, sipped his Irish coffee and exhaled a long sigh. He slid his glasses down the bridge of his nose and rubbed his eyes, stifling a yawn. The door creaked open behind him.

"Father O'Malley?" asked the voice, but he was too tired to look around.

"I am sorry my son, the service is in intermission for a little while. I'll be out soon."

It was then Father O'Malley smelt something he had not smelt within the walls of his Finchley church in some time: cigarette smoke. He twisted in his chair to look but was greeted by an empty room and a cigarette in mid-air smoking itself. Father O'Malley gawped, wide-eyed in astonishment: "It's you!"

"Mind if I close the door?" said Hal from the other side of the room.

"Yes, but of course." Father O' Malley pushed his glasses back into position, his eyes darting around the empty space at the source of the voice.

"Don't worry, I am still here."

"What can I do for you? I mean, how can I serve you? What I meant to say is..."

"I was just passing," Hal interrupted.

"Oh, so you were just passing? I see, so you like to pass through Finchley?"

"Always."

"Oh."

"Get some smokes, you know."

"You need to get what?"

"Smokes"

"You... er... smoke?"

"Sure I do."

"Do you drink too?"

"Wouldn't trust a man who doesn't, Father."

"Oh, well, they do, you do say eat drink and be merry, I guess."

"I get my smokes from Booze and Mags while on the way to the Bandy Legs to meet Keith." Hal looked at Father O'Malley's shocked expression and paused. "Oh, sometimes I forget. You can't see me can you?" Father O'Malley slowly shook his head.

"This goes no further than these four stone walls, right?"

"You have my absolute word, on this bible itself, so you do." Father O'Malley clutched a bible, pressing his right hand onto it. Hal materialised on the other side of the room in the Chesterfield chair, invisibility OFF. Father O'Malley gaped in awe.

"Pretty amazing huh?" said Hal with a tired, faint smile.

"Yes, yes it is... amazing." Father O'Malley was transfixed: "So you're The Holy Ghost?"

"I am just a man; it's this that does it all." Hal gestured to the suit: "Found her at some kind of crash site, several days ago."

"Where?"

"Trent Park Golf Course, seventeenth hole. I was a little drunk."

"Oh."

"I've ruled it out of being Chinese. I'm pretty sure it's alien. One press of this button renders me invisible, it gives me additional strength too." Hal paused in thought looking at the floor. There was a long silence.

"You've done all those things on the news in that?"

"Some of them, yes." Hal continued to look at the floor, he was tired. "Some of them, no."

"Why have you come here?"

"I am giving up."

Father O'Malley fell silent.

Hal took a sip of tea: "A couple of nights back, I saw a homeless man being assaulted. No one else was around so I intervened. I don't know why I said it. Only wanted something scary to say to those punks, so I put the fear of God into them, literally. After that, well, it got kinda fun, playing the superhero. I am fifty-two and a superhero. That's a way to see out a redundancy. Now there are people flying from Lourdes to London to see miracles, it's all over the TV, radio, newspapers. There's a one million pound newspaper ransom and I even have followers that call themselves frigging disciples. No offence Father."

"None taken."

"And you know what it's like to be a superhero? In real life?" Hal was wistful, looking up for a while "You feel... at your optimum. Now four men are blind, there's social unrest and I don't know what I am doing anymore."

"Well, you must do what feels right."

"I could have gleaned that from a fortune cookie."

"I read this morning that crime numbers are at the lowest since records began. The police are literally eating bagels and playing cards they have so little to do and I know this as there are several in my parish. A man who was about to commit suicide lives and, because of you, five unsolved murders have now been brought to book. I've seen a lot in my time but what you are doing my boy, well that is something else."

"What are you saying?"

Father O'Malley took off his glasses: "There are so many bible stories I could quote right now about overcoming adversity, about the will of the few versus the might of the many but that would be in my official capacity. You want to hear what I think?" Father O'Malley paused. "I think, it doesn't matter, not one jot. The fact that you exist in itself is inspiring people to be better.... On my walk in today, people I did not even know said hello to me and offered me free food, so they did.

"They're just cashing in the goodwill chips to avoid the wrath, of me."

"They are trying…. Listen, I don't even know your name."

"I never said it."

"They're trying…"

"Impersonation of a deity is bad for your health."

"Yet you still do it. Given the entire tree of decisions which you could make, you use that thing you're wearing to do good, when evil is your easiest option."

"I am really no saint Padre, the wife would tell you that."

"Nobody is," Father O'Malley smiled. The door creaked opened. Margaret and Maude, his elderly volunteer stewards, peered into the room.

"Father O'Malley, you won't believe it, the hall is full again," Margaret said, smiling.

Maude sniffed the air, smelling the cigarette smoke, both ladies focused on Hal staring at the floor then at Father O'Malley, trying to ascertain what seemed wrong in this scene.

"We are sorry to interrupt," added Margaret. "We'll be right outside."

"Thank you ladies, I'll be there soon. That will be all." Margaret and Maude closed the door, disappearing down the stone corridor.

"Father O'Malley's smoking again," Margaret whispered.

"Must be the stress," Maude nodded.

Back in Father O'Malley's private room, Hal pressed the lapel button: Invisibility ON.

The wooden door opened: "Just think about it. You can see me anytime, if you want to," Father O'Malley said into thin air. With the door open, the sound of the distant crowd in the main hall grew louder.

"Think your flock is getting restless?"

"You're an unlikely hero," Father O'Malley replied, but Hal was gone.

Father O'Malley stepped out to greet his latest congregation. Amidst the hundreds of new faces, one lady in a fuchsia twin set, sprayed her perfume atomiser at the vagrant stood next to her. It was Trina.

Hal took the suit home. "Darcy?" he called out as he walked through the grass towards his small wooden out-house home. There was no response. He pressed his thumb on the fingerprint recognition unit, entered and slid off his alien attire carefully returning it to its special hanger. He took one last look around and pulled the power lever. With a final surge, the room fell silent. The monitors went black and the suit hung in shadow. He dressed himself in regular slacks and a shirt and sealed the heavy shed door shut. Hal spent the rest of his afternoon by the Meerkat enclosure at London Zoo. But instead of watching his playful, furry companions, he found himself observing the passers-by: the children playing and the large packs of tourists digitally documenting everything, including their own documentation. Two Buddhist monks in orange robes passed a couple wearing 'I Heart HG' T-shirts. Hal wondered what they made of it all. What they thought of his charade? "No more," he said softly. No one heard.

That evening, Hal found himself in the Bandy Legs, ale of the week in hand, on a barstool next to Keith. He carefully positioned himself away from the television to avoid the 24-hour rolling news coverage.

"Can't you turn that junk off, Ted?" he asked the landlord.

"Are you sick or something? This is the Second Coming. This is the Trinity."

Hal had never recalled a time when Ted had been animated over anything other than being short-changed.

"How's redundancy?" asked Keith.

"Good days and bad days."

Keith noticed Hal's bruises: "What the hell happened to you?"

"One of the bad days." Hal tried to smile. "Don't worry about it."

"Have you seen what is...?" Keith pointed to the TV.

"Yeah," Hal interrupted. "How's the family?"

"Kids are great Hal, not really kids anymore though; wife's alright, it's Jim that's not good. Tracy isn't responding to the chemo. She hasn't got long. Jim was kinda hoping that Holy Ghost might visit and use his healing touch; he's even given up the alcohol and cigarettes. Right now he's at that site in Camberwell."

"No, he should stay with her," said Hal placing his head in his hands. "He should stay."

"She was a great girl. I might go visit, but always had this thing about hospitals."

Ted turned up a news item, which drowned everything, including the noise from the fruit machine, out.

"The kidnapper has stated that if The Holy Ghost does not manifest by midnight, the girl will be shot dead."

"Will you look at that, the world's gone crazy!" Keith looked tense.

Hal took another sip of beer, trying to avert his eyes from the screen.

The report continued: "The kidnapper is believed to be a man called Richard Park. Police marksmen have surrounded the kidnapper's property in Highgate."

A large woman with several gold chains screamed repeatedly: "She disappeared last night and now this? Please Holy Ghost, if you are up there, please help my baby, please, please!"

Hal averted his eyes, but caught something on the screen which made him freeze.

"You gotta be kidding me."

"I reckon he may get more than what he bargained for that man eh, Hal? Hal?" Keith turned to an empty seat and Hal rushing out of the door: "Hal, you've left your pint! See that Ted? He's left his pint."

"He's been acting awful strange of late."

"How so?"

"It's not even last orders."

Hal hared through the quiet suburban crescents and alleys wheezing and coughing with every step, collapsing against a road sign. "Last time," he forced out in between breaths. Everything was tougher without the physical support of the suit. He approached his house, turned the key and ran straight through past a kneeling Trina surrounded by candles. From his actions the previous night he was prepared for a storm but had no time to argue. Trina's eyes followed him as he darted out of the patio door and across the garden towards his favourite place. Then her eyes narrowed.

With the lights at 13 Clifton Terrace all out, Hal placed his thumb across the fingerprint recognition scanner. With a bleep, the door unlocked and opened. He powered up the shed.

"Did you miss me?" he said looking at the hanging suit bathed in shafts of light. It had seen better days, and so had Hal. He carefully removed it from the hanger and slid it on once more, the suit snaking up his body.

Stepping into his rusty Scimitar in the lane behind the shed, he put his foot down hard. The car screeched away and weaved through the North London streets accompanied by the repeated RP sound of: "She sells sea shells on the sea shore." Terminating Trina's elocution CD, he found the news: "...and police marksmen have surrounded the grounds of the Highgate house. We haven't heard any word from inside but officers are believed to be in communication with Park. We're camped several streets away."

The car came to a halt in a quiet lane in between Highgate and Hampstead Golf Clubs. Killing the engine, he looked tentatively at the suit in his rear-view mirror: "If this doesn't work out for any reason," he said softly and earnestly, "it's been nice working with you." He found himself welling up for a second with a heavy feeling. Taking a deep breath, he pressed the lapel button: Invisibility ON. Opening the driver's door, he crept through the woodland in near silence. In the nearby streets, a crowd of hundreds had gathered holding candles. At the vanguard stood the ladies of the Finchley and Totteridge Renaissance Society and amateur paparazzi Mr Singh.

Hal bypassed the throng to reach the press area. The operation was already on a vast scale. The global press were everywhere. Journalists rehearsed pieces to camera, some already live on television. Hal eavesdropped on a reporter and her camera team.

"What if it's some kind of tabloid trap, they still haven't got a picture of He yet?"

"What if He doesn't show?"

"I'd be more worried if He does."

Hal sighed and continued stealthily past, gaining line of sight of the house. The property was large, surrounded by beautiful grounds with fountains on either side. The lights were off within, the building illuminated by several large police lights. The hostage negotiator hunched over a phone, crushing an empty coffee cup.

"He's giving us nothing until Him upstairs turns up."

By his side stood several armed police with Tasers, sub-machine guns and thermal imaging goggles. Hal felt a Pavlovian shiver.

In the distance, the crowd began to chant: "Let him through." Several officers hurriedly peeled away from the grounds towards the cries. The crowd had multiplied tenfold. By the police barricade several streets away from the house. Stood an unusual man. He had a serene quality, was in his mid-thirties and wore white robes which reached the floor. With his long hair, beard, piercing blue eyes and sandals, by all accounts, the man looked like Jesus. He stood, arms outstretched, beckoning the officers. The crowd virulently jeering the police force ahead of him.

"Please, let me speak to him," the man said softly and kindly to the police officers.

"Get back, this is a police matter, Sir."

"But you know who I am," the robed man said calmly.

"Please get to the side of the road, Sir," replied the constable nervously.

"Let him in," the crowd chanted, changing to "Let Jesus in."

Over the talkback system, an unexpected order was given. The constable stepped aside and the robed man was let through. He strolled slowly with arms outstretched past the police cordon, through the grounds with a small army of police looking on. He continued until he was stood on the lawn facing the building.

"Richard, it is I, please lay down your arms," the robed man said calmly.

The door of the house slowly creaked open. "Richard, I know you can hear me. Peace is the only way. Come with me to pray Richard." The robed man's entire demeanour conveyed benevolence. "Come on. Come on now," he called as if summoning a pet.

Hal manoeuvred closer to the building. A figure stepped out of the shadow of the doorway holding an automatic rifle and a human shield. The figure was recognisable from the television broadcast as Richard Park. However, his hostage, screaming terrified, was Hal's neighbour, Darcy. Park took one look at the robed man on the lawn, sneered and buried a shot into the Jesus lookalike's right shoulder, forcing him to the deck.

"Help me!" screamed Darcy.

"Oi! I am losing blood here!" The Jesus lookalike shouted, writhing in agony on the grass, reverting to his usual cockney accent.

Park turned his high-powered rifle onto the four large police work lights, blasting each lamp with deadly accuracy. The grounds fell immediately into darkness. Darcy screamed again as she was pulled back into the house, the door violently slamming shut.

"I want the main event, not the warm-up act!" Park slammed down the phone and watched the live television feed to see the robed man stretchered away by paramedics.

"Don't worry baby," Park said, pressing his gun to Darcy's temple. "It'll be over soon enough, one way, or another."

Darcy wept, desperately trying to wriggle free.

"Do you want sooner eh? You want sooner? Is that it?" Tears streamed down Darcy's cheeks. "Is that what you want?"

"No."

"Is that want you want?" Park looked at the time and began to whisper in her ear: "The Lord is my rock, my fortress and my deliverer; my God is my rock, in whom I take refuge. He is my shield and the horn of my salvation, my stronghold. I call to the Lord, who is worthy of praise, and I am saved from my enemies."

The police PA system was now in constant communication, but Richard wasn't listening, nor was he alone.

In the corner of the room, unseen by all, stood Hal Maybury atop a table looking down over Park and Darcy. He stood watching, judging the distance between Park and Darcy, then spread his arms. Processing an instant recall of all the wrestling he had ever consumed on Dickie Davis' World of Sport, Hal launched his rotund frame high into the air. On hearing the table creak, Park immediately emptied two shots into the room. A second later an invisible force collided with him so hard it knocked him to the ground. "Bingo," said Hal; it felt like the right thing to say, he didn't know why.

Hal lay on top of Park, wheezing, fighting for breath. Park's lucky shots had struck the suit in the chest in the same spot as from his assault in Camberwell. His magic suit flashed in between transparency and visibility, at random allowing Park a chance to see his assailant.

"You are not He," Park mumbled under the heavy mass of the visible and invisible Hal sitting on his chest.

"Indeed," Hal sighed punching Park in the face until he was unconscious. He wasn't feeling biblically wordy. He pushed the gun out of reach and rose on his invisible knees, groaning. The shells trapped in the hexagonal material in Hal's chest fell to the floor. Hal alternated in and out of visibility. Wheezing, he collapsed to the floor in agony.

"Mr Maybury?" Darcy cried: "What are you doing here?"

Hal struggled for breath: "When you hit early retirement, you can find yourself with a lot of free time on your hands."

"It's you? You're The Holy Ghost?"

Hal checked the damaged suit but the strong bulletproof material had saved him once again. He looked at Darcy trembling.

"They'll be coming." Hal grabbed his chest, heaving.

"Mr Maybury?"

"Stay, you're safe now." Hal sensed the incoming forces of the law and took a final look at the clock. The hand moved onto midnight. He scuttled down the stairs into the wine cellar. What would Charlton do in this situation, he wondered.

Armed police burst through the front doors into the house, quickly siphoning through the back doors seconds later. They discovered Park knocked out with no other sign of entry and Darcy looking at the stairwell leading to the cellar. Hal heard multiple footsteps creaking on the floor above. The suit fizzed and crackled, malfunctioning.

Hal lay in the corner of the cellar against the wall. He knew it was a matter of time before he would be discovered. The rows and rows of wine formed long, dark corridors. The faint crackle of police communications systems and footsteps from the room above became louder. He looked for any other exit, but there appeared to be only one, the way he came in. He tried the lapel button once again. It was unresponsive. He sat for a while then grabbed a tester bottle of wine at the end of the rack, which had been previously opened, and took a swig. Wine almost fit for a king he thought, almost. The police began to make their way down the cellar steps, the wooden stairs creaking as they descended. Hal looked at the broken button once more, then down the top of the suit and in the darkness amidst his fibrous grey chest hairs he noticed some brightly coloured broken glowing cables. They felt organic, not electronic. Carefully, he tried to reunite the cables with one hand, the other pressing the lapel. The police continued down the steps, slowly, cautiously, searching with their torch-mounted rifles. With shaky hands, Hal tried repeatedly to marry the cables, his breathing fast, desperate. A torchlight swept along the near wall, closer and closer. Hal reached in again, pressed the button and closed his eyes. The torchlight moved onto him. Through his closed eyelids he felt the heat of the beam. Sweat dripped from his forehead. The light stayed on him.

"Clear," said the officer and slowly walked back up the stairs. Hal sighed and looked down: Invisibility ON. Then he gasped in relief, the gasp and his shaky hands disconnecting the organic cables: Invisibility OFF. Hal sat for a while on the concrete floor looking out across the shelves of bottles wondering what it was all about, thinking of nights and adventures past. "Thank you," he said to the suit. As he sat on the floor, legs spayed out, paunch in between, Hal felt unusually at peace. He decided to finish the tester bottle; it would have been rude not to.

The following morning, Father O'Malley was hurriedly ironing his shirt in his small office, when he heard a knock at the door.

"There's no service till 9am," he replied, working the steam button into the collar.

Hal opened the door, dressed in jeans. Both men studied each other for a moment.

"So you didn't give up I see," Father O'Malley smiled.

"Guess not."

"It's early, please have a seat."

But Hal remained in the doorway: "I'm not staying."

"Oh, you're not wearing it."

"Little malfunction, left her in a safe place. Now comes the hard part, to fix her. Not sure if my telecommunications experience stretches as far as alien technology but might as well give it a try." Hal raised his Homebase carrier bag clinking with newly acquired tools. "Anyway, I better go, just checking in."

"Anytime my friend."

Hal made his way out and then stopped. "Still don't believe in any of this, you know, Him upstairs stuff, that ain't changed. I'm just your regular guy in decline with secret identity issues and an alien suit."

"Of course, what can I call you?"

"You do that Hippocratic Oath stuff right?"

"Oath of the confessional?"

"That'll do." Hal paused and had a scratch "Hal, my name is Hal."

"Connor. You know some good has come out of this, so it has. Street Spirit is back at number one." Father O'Malley smiled. Hal looked blank. "It's a record," he added but Hal was still blank. "I'll see you later, mysterious ways and all that."

"See you later, Father."

The streets were quiet. Mr Singh of Booze and Mags waved to Hal in passing. The kids in the street were arguing: "I'll be the kidnapper."

"No, I'm the kidnapper."

"I'm going to use my '+10 condemned to Hell attack', yeah, then you'll know what time it is."

"I'm going to use my Vishnu block."

"What's a Vishnu block?"

"It is written."

As Hal approached his Finchley home, he became paralysed by a sudden bad feeling. As he withdrew his keys, he smelt smoke. Looking up, smoke was billowing over his roof in the breeze. He forced the keys into the lock, swinging the door open and hurried inside. The house was safe, but as Hal walked through the kitchen to the patio he saw Trina in the garden wearing an immaculate long white dress and flat white shoes. She held a wooden torch aloft. At the back of the garden was raging fire, spitting cinders of wood and ash. The shed was ablaze. Hal rushed toward it but was beaten back by the heat of the flames.

"Trina! What have you done?"

"He is close Hal," she said, holding the lit torch.

"Who is?"

"The Holy Ghost. I needed to shield you from your vices."

"What?"

"Alcohol, smoking, television."

"Oh no," Hal said sadly. Trina began to pray and held her hand on his head. Hal darted to the rusty spigot, attached a hose and slowly turned it.

"He is coming Hal."

The spigot finally released some water but the pressure was pathetic. Hal watched the shed burn and dropped the hose.

"Mr Maybury!" Darcy shouted as she ran into the garden, but Hal stood unable to move, the shed burning in broad daylight in front of his eyes.

"Mr Maybury? You can stop it."

"I can't, I can't." Hal inhaled the smell of petrol fumes and burning wood. The fire was intense, even parts of the fence had caught alight.

Hours later, when the fire services departed, Hal checked the wreckage. There was no suit or casket in the shed, just cinders and rubble.

"It was for the best," Trina repeated earnestly. "He is back."

Trina mumbled fervently in Hungarian whilst Hal gazed at his reflection in the charred broken mirror for perhaps longer than he should.

"And so it was," he said quietly. Tabitha, the cat, rubbed herself against his legs, purring.

The separation was swift, possibly the most amicable exchange in their short marriage. Hal left 14 Clifton Terrace to Trina. He became a lodger in the attic room of a young, trendy Buddhist couple in Chalk Farm. A whole month had passed and The Holy Ghost hysteria had gradually died down. Global economics was once again at the forefront of the news. It had also been a month since Hal had touched alcohol, although at times he missed it. He spent the majority of his days at his favourite place which he'd discovered on his invisible journeys: The Caribbean Centre in Camden. Lodged above a shop, he played out the days playing dominoes, eating plantain and rice and soaking up the laughter. The well-dressed gentlemen of the Caribbean Centre were always laughing and quickly accepted Hal, but everyone knew that he carried with him a sense of emptiness and loss that no one could quite explain.

It was a Friday night where, during a game of gin-rummy, came a knock at the door. Harp, the Antiguan, ambled over to answer it.

"Who there?" Winston asked, sneaking a quick look at Hal's hand.

"Wait man!" Harp called along into the corridor looking down. Then he turned back to the table: "Hal, it's for you."

"Must be the wrong address."

"I don't think so."

"Don't look at my cards," Hal smiled to Winston as he placed his hand face down and walked over to the doorway. As he got there, he stopped dead in his tracks. For in the doorway on the floor lay a charred metallic box. It was unmistakably the burnt casket from the crater.

"Harp, who left this?"

"Some long man left it and walked away."

Hal kneeled and popped open the lid. It slowly opened, the inside of the casket was untouched and in the centre of it the suit looking as good as new, folded and lit by the golden rim light of the casket.

"Wha' that?" asked Harp, looking at the strange metallic box.

"What did the man look like?" replied Hal.

"Only saw him from behind. Some long man in a black coat. Real tall, you won't miss him."

Hal grabbed the suit, tucked it under his arm and ran down the corridor.

"I take it you're out of this round?" shouted Winston after him.

Hal darted down the stairs and burst through the door onto street level, looking both ways. Underneath a handmade 'Alcoholic Research' signpost, he saw Horace, the homeless man, once again. Horace took one look at Hal and pointed towards the park. Hal threw whatever monetary shrapnel was to hand into his lap and ran as best he could until he arrived at the park gates. On the other side, in the distance, a very tall man strode across the dark grass.

"Wait!" Hal called but the giant man kept walking. It took Hal three attempts to get his large frame over the railing and he wheezed and wretched. Then he looked at the suit and put it on. It slid up him. Hal began to run.

With added speed, he gained on the giant figure: "Wait, please!" he cried. The giant discarded his long, black coat on the grass but kept walking.

"Please!" Hal called out. The giant stopped in the centre of the grass and turned. His face was a plastic mask and he was wearing an identical suit to Hal's.

"You're from up there aren't you? The crash site at the golf course?" Hal pointed towards the light-polluted sky.

"We are indeed from a distant galaxy Hal, but nothing crashed." The giant took off his hat and gloves. He had no hands, and no face. Slowly, the giant removed his shoes, leaving the appearance of an invisible body inhabiting a visible suit. Hal reached out, passing his hand through the head. There was nothing there.

"Not all life in the universe looks the way you'd expect it to Hal," the suit replied. Hal found himself rubbing his suit once again for reassurance. It took him a moment to thoughtfully look at his own attire.

"Is it?" he said looking down.

"Yes, she is alive and fully functional."

Hal noticed additional buttons on his wrists.

"What do these do?"

"You'll find out soon enough," the giant suit replied. "I must return."

"Wait. Why me? Why did you bring it back to me?"

"We're watchers. We don't normally intervene," the giant paused and said softly with a smile: "But, well, you're good to watch, Hal."

The earth began to shake violently all around him. Hal was thrown to the floor then found himself falling, rocks colliding all about him. The alien suit waved goodbye and disappeared deep into the earth. When Hal opened his eyes, he discovered himself once again at the bottom of a canyon, with steep rock walls billowing with steam and the faint smell of sulphur escaping from vents in between the rocks. Where the alien suit had stood and disappeared seconds before lay a fluttering white stack of paper. Hal moved closer over to it and picked it up. It was a newspaper with the headline:

'WHO IS DIABLO?'

Below the headline was an article on a new super-criminal with a propensity to make things burn. Hal folded up the paper and began the ascent to the rim of the canyon. Wheezing as he reached the top, he looked back to see a grey fog roll into the canyon engulfing and circling it. With a deep tone, the canyon was gone and everything was parkland once more. Hal lay on his back on the grass looking at the night's sky.

"Mr Maybury?" said a familiar voice. Hal looked up to see Darcy, standing above him. She seemed unusually excited.

"Darcy?" Hal signed in relief; "How did you get here?"

"Look, look, the big man gave it to me," Darcy replied. Hal refocused to take a long look at her. Darcy was wearing a grey jump suit with a hexagonal pattern on it. It was identical to his.

"Thought you needed a partner."

"A what? Jesus H, I work alone. Most definitely alone." Hal rose to his feet, took one look back at where the canyon once was, then slowly strolled back towards the gate. Darcy followed.

"What was that hole?" she asked.

"I don't really know."

"You wanna cigarette?"

"Haven't I told you about that already?"

"Think we need a bigger shed, Hal?"

"It's Mr Maybury to you."

"Mr Maybury, I was thinking of a name, what do think my

name should be? What about Archangel of Death? Do you like that? I like that. This is going to be totally awesome you know, you and me. Fighting crime, pow-pow," she said making martial arts moves.

Hal walked determinedly back towards the park gates and looked across the North London skyline, but a smile crept slowly across his face.

"Pow-pow." Who'd have thought?

THE END